THE HEART OF INNOCENCE

AMISH HEARTS SERIES, BOOK 1

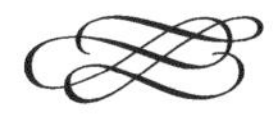

GRACE LEWIS

BOOK DESCRIPTION

Jamesport, Missouri, early 1980s.

Betsie Hershberger's whole world is her little Amish village and her small family. The youngest of four sisters, she is the apple of their eye, and privy to all their secrets. When the circus comes to town, Betsie's overactive imagination risks getting her eldest sister in trouble, and harming an innocent friend.

Sarah Hershberger is responsible for her sisters since their mother's death. Her father, Leroy, relies on her to keep track of the house and his willful daughters while he works on the farm, but Sarah fears this dependence will leave no room for her to make a family of her own. Proving this fear well founded, Leroy detests the only man Sarah loves and forbids marriage.

Will Betsie save the day? Will Sarah convince her father to grant her the love she seeks? Or will the sisters end up in more trouble than they bargained for?

~

The Heart of Innocence is the first book in the *Amish Hearts* series (the prequel to the *Amish Sisters* series). Each book is a stand-alone read, but to make the most of the series you should consider reading them in order.

FOREWORD

This book is dedicated to you, the reader.

Thank you for taking a chance on me, and for joining me on this journey.

Do you want to keep up to date with all of my latest releases, and **start reading *Secret Love* and *River Blessings*, exclusive spinoffs from the *Amish Hearts* and the *Amish Sisters series*, for free?**

Join my readers' group (copy and paste this link into your browser: *bit.ly/Grace-FreeBook*). Details can be found at the end of the book.

"Behold, children are a heritage from the LORD; the fruit of the womb is a reward."
~ Psalm 127:3

TALL TALES

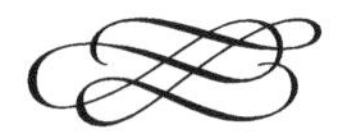

"People are convinced he will win the nomination," Benjamin Lambright said. "Can you imagine it? Ronald Reagan, the next President of the United States, a movie star!" He hooked his thumbs in his suspenders and gave Betsie a teasing wink.

"Ben," Sarah Hershberger said. "You're boring her with your political talk."

"He's not!" Betsie cried.

Betsie Hershberger was a lot of things, but she was not a stupid child, and she disliked being treated like one. At eleven she was the shortest girl in her class, but she could outsmart them all at mathematics. She hitched up her school satchel, her brown curls bouncing on her back as she tried to keep up with the large strides of her adult companions. It was early morning, and the woods were cool. The sun winked at them through the leaves, its warmth hinting at the heat they could expect later in the day. Sarah and Ben were walking her to school. Normally Betsie wouldn't have wanted anyone to walk her anywhere, but this provided Sarah and Ben an opportunity to meet, and Betsie couldn't deny them that.

Benjamin Lambright worked on an *Englischer* farm on the other side of the river that marked the boundaries of the Amish village, so he found time for Sarah only in the early hours before the day started, and late at night when the day had finally come to a close. It also happened to be the only time Leroy Hershberger couldn't spot them together. Father of the Hershberger girls, he disapproved of Ben, much to Betsie's confusion.

Betsie thought about what Ben had said. She had never seen a Ronald Reagan movie, but her sister Kathy loved him. She had a secret stash of magazines under her bed. He was certainly handsome, but was that enough to make a good president? She wondered if Ben was pulling her leg, but she didn't think he would make a joke at her expense. Ben wasn't like most adults, he was funny and attentive, and he took her seriously.

"Ben." Betsie frowned. "Can you vote?"

"*Nee*." Ben shrugged.

"Why not?"

"It goes against the *Ordnung*," Ben explained, scratching the back of his tanned neck. They walked out of the woods into a large clearing where a squat school building stood in the middle. Betsie saw her classmates milling about the yard. "Besides, I don't have any interest in politics. I just pick up a lot of news from my *Englischer* boss."

"Useless information," Sarah muttered under her breath, tucking a loose strand of blond hair behind her ears. Betsie giggled.

"Well." Ben tilted his head, a furtive smile on his handsome face. "Not all information is useless. I have one interesting thing you might want to know."

"Humph." Sarah rolled her eyes.

"Would you like to know, beautiful Betsie?" Ben asked.

"*Ja!*" Betsie bounced on the balls of her feet.

"The circus is coming to town next week. Would you like to go?"

"The circus!" Betsie clapped her hands. "Can we go, Sarah? Can we?"

Sarah bit her lip, a sure sign that she was reluctant to agree. Her pale oval face was still, but her heavily lashed eyes darted from Ben to Betsie, agitated at the decision she had to make.

"They have clowns, cotton candy, and all sorts of animals doing tricks. James was telling me they even have an anaconda from the rainforest."

"What's an anaconda?" Betsie asked, her eyes so similar to Sarah's, wide with wonder.

"It's the largest snake in the world. It can grow as tall as the length of your fields."

Betsie's mouth hung open in shock.

"They even have motorized rides and," Ben grinned down at Sarah, "they even have Twinkies."

Sarah loved Twinkies but could never buy any from town. *Daed* didn't approve of Twinkies, just like he didn't approve of Ben Lambright. Sarah tried not to smile, but Ben's grin demanded reciprocation.

"Oh, all right," Sarah said. "But you have to promise not to tell *Daed* we found out from Ben." She paused and added, "Because if you do, he'll be furious with me." She was serious now.

"You know I won't tell." Betsie was earnest.

"Now run along and learn something," Sarah said, pushing Betsie gently.

"Unless you want to be like Sarah here," Ben said, tapping his finger against Sarah's temple.

"Ben," Sarah protested, swatting his hand away, but she was grinning and there was a warm glow in her eyes.

Betsie ran off in the schoolyard's direction, her satchel bouncing against her thin hips. At the edge of the yard, she looked back at the woods. Ben and Sarah were walking back up the path, fractured sunlight bouncing off their heads, their hands – one pale and delicate, the other tan and firm – held firmly together.

Betsie smiled at the sight and turned to join her friends. She knew Sarah and Ben loved each other very much. It was a shame that *Daed* didn't approve. Because of that, Sarah had to pretend she wasn't walking out with anybody. Betsie didn't understand why *Daed* disliked Ben so much, but she knew it would be stupid to ask him to change his mind. The last time anyone had mentioned Ben in the house, their father hadn't eaten supper or breakfast the next day.

Shaking her head to dismiss her thoughts, Betsie walked into the schoolyard. The younger children were playing a game of tag, while the eldest sat in groups, looking about the yard as if they were too old for such behavior. A large group of pupils was crowded around one of the benches in the yard, watching something Betsie couldn't see. The only person not interested in the gasping crowd close beside them was Samuel King. He was busy fixing a yellow pinwheel, his chestnut hair glowing fiery bronze under the morning sun.

"Betsie! Look at what I found," Susan Hostetler, a tall girl with buck teeth, stood at the heart of the crowd. She waved at her. Betsie came closer and her heart stopped for a moment. A snake was twisted around Susan's arm; a line of turmeric yellow ran through its khaki green scales. Betsie recognized it as a garden snake. You could easily find one near the woods and the river where they feasted on frogs. It was beautiful.

"It's just a common garden snake," Betsie said, flipping her hair behind her shoulders. "What's so special about that?"

"You're just jealous," Susan accused her.

"Jealous? Me?" Betsie's laugh was high and melodious. "Why would I be jealous of a common garden snake when an anaconda nearly killed me?"

The crowd gasped. Betsie was enjoying the attention. That would show up prissy Miss Susan for calling her jealous.

"That's a lie! You're a liar," Susan said.

"*Nee*," Betsie said with grave dignity. "It's no lie. I saw one at the circus when I was a *kinner*." Everyone was staring at her, waiting for her to continue. She smiled a little to herself. "I was only four, but I still remember the lights and the clowns. *Daed* bought me a cotton candy, and it was so sweet. But I got lost and wandered inside a tent. It was dark, and no one was there… or so I thought."

They were hanging on her every word. Even Susan seemed to have forgotten to look skeptical. Only Samuel King seemed indifferent to the whole affair. He hadn't even looked up once from his pinwheel, but Betsie didn't pay him much thought; no one ever did.

"The first thing I felt were the floorboards trembling," Betsie whispered, and the crowd leaned in closer. "The slithering movement echoed in the darkness. Then, suddenly, something brushed against my legs; something cold and clammy and HUGE!"

They all jumped back. Susan clutched her chest, the garden snake still twisted around her arm. Betsie stopped herself from laughing out loud. She loved captivating an audience.

"Before I knew what was happening it had twisted around my legs, and its tongue was hissing in my face," Betsie said.

"Did it bite you?" Nancy, a girl from the first form, asked. "Did you die?"

"Of course she didn't die," Mathew, a boy from the seventh form, snapped. "She's standing in front of you, isn't she?"

"How did you escape?" Susan asked.

"I was very lucky," Betsie said. "The lion in the next tent roared so loudly that the snake stopped what it was doing, giving me enough time to jam my cotton candy in the anaconda's mouth and poke a finger in one of his eyes. Then I ran and ran till I found my *Daed*."

"You were so brave!"

"Did it hurt after?"

"What color was he?"

"Did they kill it for trying to eat a little girl?"

"How big was it?"

"Was it as big a liar as you are?"

Betsie's smile faded. Isaac Hilty, tall, broad, and unpleasant, was sneering at her from amongst the crowd. His friends, the two Marks, Wittmar and Graber, mirrored his expressions.

"You've never been to a circus," Isaac said. "You just couldn't stand not being the center of attention, so you lied. *Gott* is watching Betsie Hershberger, and *Gott* will punish your sins!"

Betsie felt a retort rising up her throat, but she knew better than to argue with Isaac Hilty. In the senior-most class, Isaac was a mean boy who took pleasure in condemning them all to damnation for as little as forgetting to clear pencil shavings off the schoolroom floor.

"Admit it!" Isaac said, pointing an accusing finger at Betsie. "Admit your sin of lies and pride!"

Betsie was hopping mad. How dare Isaac Hilty make a spectacle of her? She decided to throw caution to the wind and tell him exactly what she thought of him. Yes, Isaac would complain to a teacher and then to her father, but it was only a minor story. How bad could the punishment be?

"It's not a lie."

Betsie, along with everyone in the yard, swung her head towards the boy sitting in the grass fixing the pinwheel. Samuel wiped his sweaty hands on his pants and then blew; the yellow paper flower became a spinning blur.

"What did you say?" Isaac asked, taking a threatening step towards Samuel.

"I said she's telling the truth," Samuel said, shrugging his shoulders. "I was there that year. They even had fireworks on the last day. I saw the anaconda, and one of the clowns told me to stay away from the tent after dark because a girl had nearly gotten eaten a few days earlier."

Betsie stared. Why was Samuel King, the boy who seldom talked to anyone because he didn't have any friends, defending her?

"You filthy little liar!" Isaac roared. He made to shove Samuel, but Betsie rushed to stand in between them.

"Leave him alone!" Betsie shouted. "You wanted the truth, and we gave it to you. Now go away or I'll tell a teacher!"

Isaac was panting, his chest rising and falling. He reminded Betsie of their angry bull, snorting and pawing the ground in the barn every morning.

"Are you sure you want to defend spineless Samuel? You wait till I tell Leroy about Ben," Isaac's smile was cruel. "I saw him walking with Sarah in the woods. Did you think we couldn't see you that far away? You'll be sorry you stood up for the likes of him."

Betsie's heart sank. Would Isaac really tell *Daed* about Ben walking with Sarah? *Daed* would be furious. Betsie considered stepping away and letting Isaac have his way with Samuel. What did Samuel mean to her anyway? Sarah would be hurt and upset if *Daed* found out about Ben, and he would refuse to take her to the circus.

But before she could decide, the school bell clanged. The crowd of pupils dispersed, and Isaac Hilty gave her one last dirty look and went to join the throng heading inside. Samuel didn't wait for her to say anything but shuffled inside as well, his shoulders hunched.

Betsie felt sorry for him. She had always thought Samuel was odd and quiet. She realized that she wouldn't have let Isaac bully him, not because giving in to Isaac's threats would have given the bully power over her, but because it was the right thing to do. Samuel had helped her out when he had no reason to. This was the least she could do.

She kept glancing at Samuel throughout the morning lessons, but he never turned to look at her once. She wanted to mouth thank you, and she expected a thank you back, but the boy refused to look anywhere but at the blackboard. Frustrated with his lack of gratitude, she tore a small piece of paper and scribbled "Thank you" on it. She folded it once, twice, thrice, then made sure all the teachers were busy.

"Pssst!" She leaned forward, waving the note in front of Samuel's face. Susan, who sat between them, stared. "Hey," Betsie whispered. "Take it! Take it!"

"Take what, Miss Hershberger?"

Miss Diane Troyer, spectacles perched on her hooked nose, looked down at Betsie. She was the strictest teacher they had, her thin mouth never lifting into a smile. She was frowning now, her hand outstretched for the note.

"Hand it over," Miss Troyer said.

Betsie did so, her heart thundering against her ribs. First Isaac threatening to tell *Daed* about Sarah and Ben, and now getting caught passing notes by Miss Troyer; she was in big trouble.

MEN'S WORK

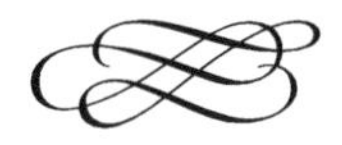

"And then she made me write a hundred lines during recess," Betsie huffed.

Her sister, Kathy, pumped water while Betsie cleaned her hands and face. She could still feel a thin residue of chalk dust all over her skin. Miriam, their other sister, was lying in the grass beside the hand pump, her hand behind her head. She was chewing on a straw of hay, her pale green eyes following the clouds.

"But that's not the worst part."

"What's the worst part?" Kathy asked. Her cheeks were flushed with the effort. She was sixteen, the most beautiful of all the sisters, with dark blue eyes in a pale heart-shaped face. She was also the most dramatic. She loved watching movies and had already watched six pictures in the first three months of her *Rumspringa.* Her *Englischer* friend, Julia, had a VCR at home, but Kathy had been too afraid to ask *Daed* for permission to go.

"Isaac Hilty said he'd tell *Daed* about Ben and Sarah," Betsie said.

Kathy gasped, her hand clutching her throat. Miriam only snorted.

"That Isaac Hilty is all bark and no bite," Miriam said. "He once said he'd tell *Daed* that I'd been picking plums from his family's gardens. I put such a fear of *Gott* in him, he was crying by the time I was done."

"But Miriam," Kathy lifted her *kapp* to scratch her sweaty scalp. "You're so brave and big. Betsie is only eleven."

"She'll be in her *Rumspringa* in another five years," Miriam shrugged. "She should learn how to hold her own ground."

Betsie thought about this as she finished scraping the last of the chalk from under her nails. Miriam was nineteen and fresh out of her *Rumspringa.* She had taken the most time out of anyone in the village before being baptized into the faith. Betsie knew it had worried *Daed,* but he had said nothing to Miriam. When it came to Miriam, *Daed* had a soft spot, and he showed lenience in most matters the others got in trouble for. Maybe it was because she had been the one who had found their mother the morning she had died.

Betsie had only been six at the time her mother had died, but she knew their mother had been ill for a long time, her health failing her day by day. Miriam had been up early that day, and she made breakfast for their mother.

Betsie could see it in her mind's eye: fourteen-year-old Miriam, tall and gangling, cooking porridge on the stove in her nightdress, her tongue sticking out of her mouth as she concentrated. She could also imagine the pride on her sister's face for finally being able to do something for their mother.

The house had woken to Miriam's wails. Their mother had passed away in the time it had taken Miriam to make porridge. Miriam hadn't cried since that day and the Hershbergers had grown an aversion to gloopy breakfast food.

"There," Kathy said, stepping back from the hand pump. "You're all clean and I'm late."

"Which movie are you going to see today?" Betsie asked.

"*The Empire Strikes Back*," Kathy said. "Julia says it is very Christian."

"Really?" Miriam chuckled in disbelief.

"Well, if you dismiss all the magic and the aliens, it's the Biblical story of overcoming evil." Kathy grinned. "Do you have five dollars?"

"Didn't you sell the eggs yesterday?" Miriam asked.

"*Ja*," Kathy said. "And I got ten dollars for them at the grocery store."

"That's enough for a movie and snacks, surely," Miriam said.

"Dolores said we might go for an early dinner afterwards at the diner," Kathy said.

"Dolores and her diner." Miriam rolled her eyes. "If she doesn't watch it, she'll be as big as her house soon."

Betsie giggled at the thought of Dolores Miller's legs sticking out of her front windows, her head pushing against the ceiling. Miriam took out her own fat wallet and handed Kathy ten dollars.

"Buy a few glazed doughnuts for Betsie," she said, winking.

"*Denke*," Kathy and Betsie said in unison.

Once Kathy left, Miriam made Betsie a few sandwiches to eat. Miriam refused to cook anything on the stove, and since Sarah was in town with *Daed* selling her quilts to a local merchant, sandwiches and fruit were all that was on offer. Betsie washed them down with a glass of milk, then stared across the table at Miriam.

"Do we have chores?" Betsie asked.

"I was supposed to mend *Daed's* socks," Miriam grimaced. "But I'd rather muck out the stalls."

Betsie made a face.

"It's not so bad," Miriam laughed. "The cows are friendly, it just the bull you have to beware of."

"It's stinky work," Betsie complained.

"At least it's proper work," Miriam said. "Come on," she urged, "We will spare *Daed* the extra chore and he'll be pleased we helped with the farm. He struggles on it alone."

Betsie bit her lip.

"But I'll ruin my dress," she said.

"Oh, I have just the thing for that," Miriam said, clapping her hands. She rushed out of the room and came back after a few minutes with a pair of old breeches and a small shirt. "These were *Daed's* when he was younger. Go on, put them on."

Betsie did as she was told. The pants felt comfortable, but she felt exposed. Miriam put on a pair of pants and a shirt as well, and they trudged out to the barn. The only time Betsie was allowed in the barn was early in the morning with Sarah to milk the cows. The bull frightened her a little with its snorting.

Daed was very strict about the chores. The girls were supposed to keep to the house and leave the fields and the barn to him. They could milk the cows, feed the hens, and collect the eggs, but the rest was a man's job, and they were not men.

Miriam handed her a small trowel and took the shovel herself. Betsie had to cover her face with a handkerchief to stop herself from gagging on the stink. They started from the back, far away from the bull, mucking out stall after stall, sweat trickling down their faces. Miriam was animated, singing songs and making jokes, and Betsie relaxed as well. The bull grunted and pawed the ground, getting agitated by the minute as they approached his stall.

Throwing caution to the wind, Betsie decided to show Miriam the trick she had learned the other day when she had been milking the cows. She walked up to the stall of Sadie, the most sweet-tempered of their cows, and dragged the milking stool by her side.

"Look, Miriam," Betsie said, climbing on top of the cow in the second-to-last stall. "I'm in the circus!"

"Be careful, Betsie," Miriam warned.

"I'm doing it! I'm doing it!" Betsie laughed, balancing herself on one leg. The cow shifted slightly and Betsie lost her balance. She swayed one way, then forward, and before she knew what was happening, she had tilted off the cow and into the next stall. Her face smacked against the sweaty hide of the bull, and she landed on her back in the vile muck on the floor.

Betsie screamed. The bull snorted and roared, its eyes rolling in its head. It backed up, ready to charge. Fear paralyzed Betsie, her eyes wide and staring, a scream lodged in her throat so she couldn't breathe.

"Betsie!" she heard Miriam scream from a great distance, but it was enough to snap her out of her trance. She ran towards the stall door. It was locked from the outside, but her adrenaline made her agile, and she jumped up till she hooked one foot over the top of the door. Scrambling with her hands and feet, she found purchase and lifted herself up just as the bull struck the door, jarring her entire body with its impact. Miriam grabbed her by the waist and pulled her down on the barn floor to safety.

"You're safe!" Miriam whispered, her voice hoarse. "You're safe!"

"What is going on here?"

Betsie's heart lurched. Leroy Hershberger, tall, blond, and frowning, stood with his arms akimbo in the barn door. His gaze took in Betsie's soiled clothes, his frown deepened, and he took a step forward. The bull slammed its horns against the stall door. Betsie screamed.

BEDTIME STORIES

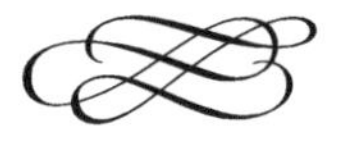

"It's not her fault, *Daed*," Miriam said. "It was my idea to clean the stalls."

"She is not a child, Miriam!" Leroy said. "She should take responsibility for her own actions."

"What's wrong?" Sarah had arrived. She took one look at Betsie's soiled breeches and their father's thunderous expression and rushed forward. "Betsie, are you okay?"

"The bull is in a fit state!" Leroy thundered. "It will take ages to calm it down."

"She was only trying to help, *Daed*," Sarah said. "You work so hard and Betsie sees how much it's affecting your health. You can't blame her for trying to lighten your load."

Leroy frowned but said nothing. He turned

towards the bull's stall and began chucking hay inside. The bull snorted, but it had calmed greatly after hearing Leroy's voice. Sarah winked at Betsie, and Betsie felt a little better about the whole incident. Miriam pushed Betsie off her lap and gestured for her to follow her outside. Betsie all but ran out of the barn, her sisters by her side.

For the rest of the day, Betsie tried to avoid Leroy as much as she could. She took a long bath and allowed Sarah to scrub her till she was pink, but she could still detect a faint smell of manure from her skin. Leroy wasn't present at dinner, so Sarah left him a plate of food in the oven. This wasn't unusual because the farm kept Leroy out of the house most nights.

Kathy came back home just after dinner, a pink box of glazed doughnuts in her hands. Betsie's mouth watered, but she ignored the box and went directly to bed. After the events of the day, she didn't think she deserved sweet treats. A part of her blamed Miriam, but if she were honest, she blamed Leroy. For as long as she could remember Leroy had been busy with the farm, spending day and night on planting, harvesting, and caring for the barn animals. His parenting was distracted, and when he did focus on his daughters, it was a harsh comment here, a snide remark there, and nothing more. The girls weren't allowed to help, so they felt isolated from their father.

Betsie wished their mother was still alive.

"Betsie?"

Sarah slid under the covers, Miriam sat on the other side, and Kathy plopped down at the foot of the bed, the box of doughnuts in her lap. She lifted the cover to show Betsie the perfectly glazed doughnuts, twinkling in the candlelight.

"I'm not hungry," Betsie said.

"Betsie not hungry for sweets?" Kathy's mouth opened in surprise. "Are you running a fever?"

"Don't be upset about what happened in the barn," Sarah said, brushing the hair off Betsie's brow.

"It wasn't your fault," Miriam said, pinching her cheek. "*Daed* knows that. He just gets agitated because of the stress he's under."

"But I added to that stress," Betsie whined. "I wanted to help take some away."

"There's what we want and what *Gott* wills." Sarah shrugged. "You can't fight against *Gott's* will."

"Besides," Kathy said, pushing the box under Betsie's nose. "You've already been punished enough today, why punish yourself some more?

Eat the doughnuts before I do!" she threatened, her smile toothy and mischievous.

Betsie took a large bite, savoring the taste of fried dough and licking the sweet glaze off her lips.

"Why doesn't he let us help?" she asked, after she had devoured the first of her doughnuts. "It's not like girls don't help around the farm and on the field. Susan helps thresh during the harvest, and she makes fun of me for being lazy."

Sarah and Miriam exchanged looks.

"Why does he hate us?" Betsie cried, her doughnut dropping out of her hand and back in its box. Kathy put the box aside and hugged Betsie. Sarah and Miriam let her cry it out, then helped her under the covers. Betsie sniffled, looking up at the faces of her sisters.

"He doesn't hate us," Miriam said. "He fears overworking us."

"It's because of *Mamm*," Sarah said, laying a cool hand on Betsie's cheek. "She used to help him out in the field and the barn. She kept working even though she grew weaker and weaker."

"He thinks he could have stopped her dying if he hadn't made her do all that work," Kathy finished.

"But that's silly," Betsie said.

"*Ja*." Miriam kissed her forehead. "But we all have silly ways of coping when our loved ones leave us." Her face looked paler in the dim light, her eyes hooded. "Don't think about it too much. I promise *Daed* will have forgotten about it by breakfast."

She waved and walked towards the bedroom door.

"Save some doughnuts for breakfast," Kathy said, getting up and following Miriam. "Don't eat them all up in the night."

Sarah tucked Betsie in and blew out the candle.

"Sarah," Betsie said, taking her sister's hand. "I have to tell you something."

Sarah sat back down, and Betsie's throat went dry. Breath felt like sandpaper rubbing against her throat.

"I did something bad today," she said, licking her lips. "I told a lie, and Isaac Hilty said he would tell *Daed* about Ben. He saw us at the edge of the woods."

Sarah sat still. Tears stung Betsie's eyes.

"It was naughty of me, and I shouldn't have," Betsie confessed, "but it was also Samuel King's fault! He shouldn't have said my lie was true. I think Isaac hated that more than anything. And then I was forced to defend Samuel, and that just made it worse!"

"Hold on," Sarah interrupted. "What lie? What are you talking about?"

Betsie told her from the beginning. Her heart raced, but she steeled herself for Sarah's cutting disappointment. She owed her sister the truth, even if it meant Sarah would hate her forever.

"It's all my fault, and I'm sorry," Betsie said in a small voice.

"Oh, Betsie," Sarah sighed. "What are we going to do with you?"

"I'll make it up to you, I promise," Betsie sobbed. "I'll go and apologize to Isaac and tell him to punish me, not you."

"You will do no such thing," Sarah said, and Betsie could make out a deep frown on her face in the moonlight. "Isaac Hilty is a bully, and Hershbergers don't give in to a bully's demands." She pinched the bridge of her nose, and Betsie knew her sister was thinking hard. "I'm not angry, and Isaac's threats don't bother me. What does bother me is that you think defending Samuel King was the wrong thing to do."

Betsie chewed the inside of her cheek.

"He's just so strange," Betsie said. "He doesn't

talk to anyone and keeps fiddling with junk. He wouldn't even take my note and that got me in trouble with the teachers!"

"Be that as it may," Sarah said, "he took your side in an argument he did not need to get into. It shows courage, and care for you, the perfect recipe for a friend."

"Like Ben?"

"Like Ben."

"Sarah?" Betsie bit her lip. "Why is Ben a secret?"

Sarah was quiet for so long, Betsie thought she would not answer.

"You remember Arthur Yoder?" Sarah asked.

"*Ja*," Betsie nodded. Arthur had been Sarah's friend. He had moved to another Amish town a few years ago. "But what does he have to do with Ben?"

"I'll explain," Sarah said. "Arthur had to move to another town because his *Daed* didn't get to inherit the farm, remember?"

"*Ja*," Betsie nodded. "Libby Yoder's *Daed* got the farm."

"Just like our *Daed* inherited this farm from *Grossdaed*." Sarah picked at a loose thread on Betsie's bedspread. "Most men only give the farm to one of their sons, the rest having to find land for themselves. The Lambright men are a bit strange like that. Ben's *Grossdaed* had five sons, and he divided his land among them. Ben's *Daed,* Obadiah, has done the same, and he has four sons of his own. That leaves Ben only a small parcel of land that he can't even erect a barn on."

"Oh," Betsie frowned. "Is that why *Daed* doesn't like him, because he doesn't have any land?"

"Partly," Sarah said. "What *Daed* dislikes is what he considers disloyalty on Ben's part. You see *Daed* in the fields, slaving away on the farm on his own. He thinks Ben should offer out his services to Amish men, on Amish farms, rather than help *Englischers* line their pockets with fat profits because they pay more."

Betsie considered this a moment and had to agree. They had been taught since they were young that community was what made the Amish way work. Everyone had to do their part or else the whole village would fail.

"*Daed* thinks he's a traitor," Betsie said.

Sarah chuckled. "*Nee,* he thinks Ben is unreliable," she shook her head, "but it's not like that at all. Ben is a proud man, he wants to be able to buy land for himself and build his own barn. The way the community works, they will provide him with funds, but Ben wants to do it on his own merit. I know that might sound arrogant, and not a trait worthy of an Amish man, but that is who Ben is, and I love him for having a purpose he's passionate about."

Betsie chewed on that information, her mind whirring over the two men and how different, yet alike, they were.

"I'll try to make *Daed* see the Ben we know, Sarah," Betsie promised. "I don't know how yet, but I'll think of something. Leave it to me."

Sarah chuckled.

"And Sarah..."

"*Ja,* beautiful Betsie?" Sarah kissed her little sister's forehead.

"Don't have more than one son, please," Betsie said. "You can have as many daughters as you want."

Sarah burst out laughing. She patted Betsie on the arm and wished her a good night. Betsie lay awake for a little while longer, a small smile playing across her lips as she thought of Sarah and Ben, and their children. She was drifting off to sleep when her mind turned to school the next day and Samuel King. Her mouth opened wide in a yawn and she snuggled deep in her pillow. She dreamed of yellow pinwheels.

A HERD OF COWS AND MILK

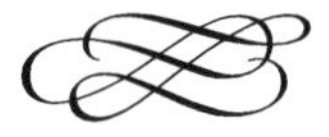

The wind was like a solid hand, slapping against her cheeks. Betsie could feel sweat trickle down her back, and she couldn't wait to get home and jump in a cool bath. Her satchel bounced against her hips as she sprinted across the Wittmar fields, but she didn't seem to notice. Her mind was on the foolish mistake she'd made during recess earlier in the day.

The entire school had been out in the yard, most of the children playing. Samuel hadn't been in school that day. Betsie had been sitting with her friends, talking about the new hymn they had learned. Isaac Hilty had been only a few feet away, talking to David Stoltzfus, a young boy Betsie's age. David was usually bright and friendly but he had looked nervous in Isaac's presence. Betsie had kept glancing in their direction, her ears pricked up when she heard them mention Samuel King.

"... you encourage him to sin," Betsie had heard Isaac saying. "You might think you're helping him, but you're only making things worse for him with *Gott*."

"It's harmless really," David had stammered. "What could a few handmade toys do?"

"It's not about what they can do," Isaac had snapped, "it's about what he will do next if this is allowed to go on."

"Why don't you worry about your own soul and leave the rest well enough alone?" Betsie had asked, her eyebrows raised archly. "I'm sure *Gott* will only judge you by your actions."

"You stay out of this if you know what's good for you," Isaac had warned.

She should have heeded the warning; she should have shut her mouth. But a deep anger had taken hold of her. She was quite sick and tired of Isaac telling everyone what to do.

"I think you're jealous," Betsie had said, rubbing her chin as if inspecting Isaac. "You're green with envy because you can't do half the things

Samuel can do. Are you saying *Gott* made a mistake giving Samuel talent?"

Isaac had taken a threatening step towards her, but the bell had rung and they had all filed inside the school. She had left quickly after the last bell had rung, dismissing the pupils for the day.

Now she was rushing home before Isaac Hilty caught up with her.

"There she is!" Mark Wittmar cried from across the field. "I told you she crosses our fields every day."

Betsie's throat constricted in panic. She ran. Heavy footsteps thundered after her. She found the dirt path and ran blindly, glancing over her shoulder to see Isaac Hilty, and the Marks, Wittmar and Graber, running after her. She faced front and put on a spurt of speed, only to smack into a cow. The collision forced her back; she lost her balance and landed on her bottom in the dirt path.

Cows lowed and came to a standstill around her. Betsie rubbed her bottom and got up. She stood amongst the herd and watched Isaac Hilty and his friends as they came cautiously forward. The village had a communal pasture near the woods, and it was common for farmers to herd their cows there according to a strict schedule. For Betsie, a herd meant an adult, and no matter how sure Isaac was of his judgment, Betsie knew he'd think twice before hitting a girl in front of adults.

"Betsie?"

A hat jammed on his auburn hair, his sleeves rolled up, Samuel King walked out of the herd and crouched down in front of Betsie. She saw him look from her to Isaac and the Marks, and understanding dawn in his hazel eyes. A calf from the herd tried to eat his hat, but he just waved its mouth away.

"*Gott* sure works in mysterious ways," Isaac tittered. "He has sent us the opportunity to chastise both culprits."

"What?" Samuel's eyes darted from the three boys to Betsie, who had come to stand beside him. The herd, deciding that the children weren't a stop for food, or remotely interesting, had moved on towards the pastures. Betsie could see Samuel's mind working behind his eyes. He was looking at the paths that led into the fields and sizing up the boys. Samuel was nothing if not resourceful.

"You can run along now, Betsie," Isaac warned.

"Let us deal with Samuel and you will be forgiven for your sins."

This was it. The choice was in front of her. Run and stay safe from the fists and ridicule of Isaac Hilty, or defend Samuel King and be condemned forever? In the end, it wasn't really a choice at all. Betsie took a step forward and stood her ground, her chin lifted in defiance.

"Don't say I didn't warn you," Isaac said, a nasty smile blooming on his lips.

He stepped forward, his eager fists coming up in front of him. Betsie tensed, her own hands going up in front of her face as both a defense and a weapon. Samuel placed a hand on her shoulder. Betsie glanced his way. He was smiling serenely.

"What's going on here?"

The growl was low and acerbic. It made Betsie's blood run cold. She whipped around so fast she cracked her neck. Melvin King was tall, his auburn beard riddled with gray strands that matched the steel gray of his eyes. He was the spitting image of Samuel, only he didn't radiate warmth like his son. Betsie had always felt skittish whenever Melvin's gaze landed on her during church services. It felt like being watched by a large, thin spider.

"I asked you a question!" Melvin barked and all the children flinched. Isaac's face drained of color, and Betsie's own teeth chattered. Melvin was not an adult you messed with under any circumstances. He had never raised his hand, nor punished anyone that Betsie knew of, but there was something forbidding about him that warned children off.

"They were just asking why I wasn't in school today," Samuel said. "They were concerned."

Samuel winked discreetly. His courage astounded Betsie. If Melvin had been frowning at her like that she wouldn't have been able to string two words together.

"They should concern themselves with their own business," Melvin spat. "My son has chores to attend to. He can't afford to go to school every day and gad about like the rest of you. Now get going!"

Isaac and his friends didn't have to be told twice. They turned and ran through the Wittmar fields. Betsie was still rooted to the ground. She wanted to run, but she was also afraid to leave Samuel alone. Her brain screamed that she was being stupid; why would Samuel be in danger alone with his own father? But a feeling at the back of her head persisted.

"And what do you need, miss?" Melvin growled, turning the force of his malevolent stare on Betsie. "A special invitation?"

"*Nee,* Mr. King," Betsie whispered, gave Samuel an apologetic look, and ran as fast as her feet could carry her. She glanced back from a safe distance. Samuel stood, his shoulders slumped, his head bent low while Melvin towered over him like a black crow superimposed upon the sun.

~

"OUCH!" Kathy hissed. "Miriam, your foot is digging in my back."

"Well, your hair is tickling my nose," Miriam sniffled.

"You're talking too loud!" Betsie warned. "*Daed* will wake up."

Kathy and Miriam settled back in Sarah's bed, Betsie between them. The moon was full tonight and bathed the floor silver. Sarah was bathed in moonlight as she looked out of the window for Ben's signal, a clutch of violets pinned to her apron. She was meeting Ben for a walk tonight and the sisters had agreed to stay up till she returned in case their father woke up and found her out of bed.

"He's late," Miriam yawned.

"Will you be back soon?" Kathy rubbed her tired eyes.

"I'll only be gone half an hour," Sarah said, distracted. "There he is!"

A wide smile bloomed across her face and it made Betsie's heart glad to see her sister so happy. Betsie wondered if she would ever find someone to love like that. She hoped so. Betsie watched Sarah go through the bedroom door and towards the kitchen, which had the only back door to the house. Sure that Sarah had gone, Betsie snuggled deep in bed. Miriam and Kathy whispered about Kathy's day in town, and Betsie felt waves of sleep stealing over her eyes.

CRASH!

Betsie sat bolt upright in bed. Miriam and Kathy had stopped breathing. They waited, not entirely sure what they were waiting for, and then the other shoe dropped. Leroy's bedroom door banged open. They heard his hurried footsteps rush to the sound of the crash.

Betsie panicked. If *Daed* caught Sarah, he would make sure Ben and Sarah never met again. She didn't think, she just jumped out of bed and tiptoed quietly towards the kitchen, where she could see a light. She peeked inside the kitchen.

Leroy, his hair disheveled, the side of his face crumpled and lined from his pillow, was looking blearily at Sarah and the stool that had fallen to the floor. Sarah was as white as a sheet, stammering incoherently.

"What are you doing in the kitchen this late at night?" Leroy asked.

"I... I... this..." Sarah stammered.

"Sarah!" Betsie wailed. She walked into the kitchen rubbing her eyes, pretending to have been disturbed in her sleep. "Is the milk ready yet?"

Leroy stared at her as if he didn't understand who she was for a minute. Sarah was just as wide-eyed and open-mouthed.

"I had a nightmare," Betsie whimpered. "I'm sorry."

Leroy frowned and looked from Sarah to Betsie.

"I was just making her some warm milk to help her fall asleep," Sarah said, finally cottoning on. "I accidentally bumped into the stool in the dark."

"Oh," Leroy said. He swayed slightly on the spot, then shook his head to regain consciousness. "Okay." He turned to get back to bed and Betsie breathed a sigh of relief. At the kitchen door Leroy stopped and turned around, a small frown on his face. He glanced at Sarah's face, then at her lapel. Betsie froze. Sarah swallowed and turned towards the stove, and Betsie hoped Leroy hadn't noticed the violets. "*Gut* night," he said, and left for bed.

"*Denke,*" Sarah whispered.

Betsie put the stool upright and waved Sarah out of the house. Her heart hammered against her ribs and she hoped their father would sleep through the night and not get suspicious. She crawled back in bed and prayed for *Gott* to forgive her lie. It was well intentioned, and she hoped it counted for something.

When she woke up in the morning, it was in her own bed. Miriam must have moved her last night. Betsie scrambled out of the covers and looked for her shoes. Did Sarah make it back alright, or did *Daed* suspect something?

She found Sarah humming as she made breakfast in the kitchen. Kathy was holding a bowl in her hands, sleeping with her eyes wide open, and, sitting beside her at the table, Miriam was rubbing her face to wake it up. Leroy was the only one wide awake, his suspicious gaze fixed on Sarah.

DINNER FOR SIX

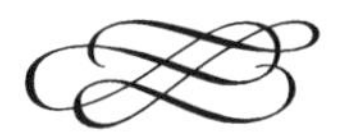

The house smelled of roasting chicken. Sarah mashed boiled potatoes with butter and chives while Miriam set the dinner table, Kathy made a pitcher of lemonade, and Betsie brought out the dinner rolls from the pantry.

Sarah wiped the fine sheen of sweat from her upper lip and glanced at the clock. It was nearly seven in the evening. *Daed* would bring in George Lengacher for dinner any minute. It had surprised Sarah when Leroy had instructed her to make a nice dinner tonight. Leroy hardly ever invited people over for a meal, especially during the summer. Sarah had pondered over who it could be all day and had been shocked to see their neighbor George Lengacher at their door.

"Why does he smell so bad?" Betsie asked, placing the rolls in a basket at the kitchen counter.

"Betsie!" Sarah admonished. "That's not a gracious thing to say."

"It's true though," Miriam said, popping a strawberry in her mouth.

"It's still not nice to say," Sarah said shortly. "And those are for dessert."

"I expect it's because he farms pigs," Kathy said, her face screwed up in deep thought. "That, and he doesn't shower much."

"Do you think the stench got to his late wife?" Miriam asked conversationally.

Sarah gaped at her sisters, horrified. Miriam had always been strange, but Kathy was becoming exactly the same. Their humor was so dry at times Sarah couldn't tell if they were joking or not. She knew it was highly inappropriate and she should put a stop to it, but she didn't have the heart to deny them the little pleasure they had in life.

After their mother had passed away Sarah was the closest thing to a maternal figure they had. Leroy's parenting was at best lenient, at worst negligent. He didn't have more than a fleeting impression of each of his daughters. He was so busy with the farm he hardly had time to be a parent.

"Can you die of bad smells?" Betsie asked. Sarah had to stop herself from laughing. There was no hint of horror in her youngest sister's eyes, just a bright curiosity. She loved Betsie dearly and took pride in her fearlessness.

"Hush, they're here!" Kathy whispered.

The front door opened and Leroy ushered George Lengacher inside. They had stepped outside to inspect the barley crop before the light faded. George sniffed and smiled at Sarah, his thin beard quivering with every twitch of his face.

"That smells delicious, Sarah," he said. His snaggletooth smile distracted from his wide nose. "I can't wait to dig in."

Sarah gave a weak smile and fetched the roasted chickens out of the oven. They said grace and dinner began. Sarah tried not to look directly across the table as she ate. Not that she disliked George Lengacher; he had been their neighbor for as long as she could remember and had been friendly and kind. It was Leroy's sudden change of heart.

Leroy wasn't a friendly neighbor. He liked to

keep himself to himself. So why the sudden warmth and the invitation to dinner? Why was he laughing at every weak joke George made and why did he keep looking at Sarah like that when George complimented her cooking or her housekeeping?

Dinner over, Sarah stacked the dishes up in the sink, ready to be washed. Water was boiling on the stove for *kaffe* and Sarah looked forward to the meal ending so she could go to bed. She was pouring *kaffe* in the mugs when Leroy walked into the kitchen, a large smile on his face.

"That was excellent, *dochder*," Leroy said, rubbing his hands in delight. "You did really well."

"I'm glad you're pleased, *Daed*," Sarah said, handing him a mug.

"I'm more than pleased," Leroy blew on the steaming liquid. "I'm thrilled and relieved. I have long worried about you and how you don't seem to attract any suitors, and after I saw you wearing flowers to bed, it broke my heart to see you slave away and not have any happiness of your own. But you don't have to worry about any of that anymore. George has agreed to marry you."

The mug Sarah was holding fell to the floor with a crash. Boiling *kaffe* splashed Sarah's shoes and soaked them. She didn't feel her skin scald; she was too worried about what her father had just said.

"What's the matter?" Leroy placed his mug on the counter and touched Sarah's arm. She could see the concern in his face but it only made her furious. How could a father be so blind to his children's desires?

"He's so old, *Daed*," Sarah said, trying hard to fight the trembling of her lips.

"*Ja*," Leroy said. "That's true. But I thought you wanted to get married. George is not the best choice but you will be next door, close to your sisters and me. He is also a kind man, which is what a woman should look for in a husband."

"But I don't want to marry for marriage's sake," Sarah protested. Tears threatened to fall, but she controlled them. "I want to marry someone I love."

The warmth left Leroy's eyes as if storm clouds had hidden the sun. His mouth pressed into a thin line.

"You're not still thinking about Ben Lambright, are you?"

Sarah pursed her lips, her gaze just as flinty as his.

"Take any thought you have of marrying Ben and put it out of your mind," Leroy said in clipped tones. "I won't give any of my daughters to a traitor like him."

"He is not a traitor."

"Isn't he? And what do you call working for *Englischer* farmers? The money he earns is tainted by *Englischer* profiteering."

"Oh, *Daed,* be realistic." Sarah tried to salvage the situation. "If taking wages from an *Englischer* is to be frowned upon than why do we sell them our eggs and milk?"

"That's different," Leroy said, his jaw jutting out.

"How is it different?" Sarah pressed on. "The *Englischer* uses the same profiteering money to buy our eggs and milk. Why is it okay for us to do this and not for Ben?"

"I will not have my *dochder* argue with me in my own home!" Leroy slapped his palm down on the counter. The mug of *kaffe* wobbled but didn't tip over. "You will not marry Ben Lambright, and that's the end of it."

"I won't marry George either," Sarah said with equal ferocity. "So you can tell him *nee*."

"Fine! Stay a spinster then, if you like," Leroy

said, turning his back to her. "I would rather see you an old maid than married to a man who will betray you for a higher profit."

Leroy stormed out of the kitchen, leaving Sarah the privacy she needed to let her tears fall.

BITTER DISAPPOINTMENT

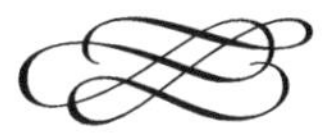

It was here. She had seen it. Red, blue, and white, the main tent was larger than anything Betsie had ever seen. The Ferris wheel touched the belly of the sky and the smell of frying food hung in the air. Betsie skipped down the path leading to the river. She had spent her morning delivering eggs to town with Kathy. She had seen the circus, and now she couldn't wait to tell everyone.

It was a Saturday and school was off for the day. The children usually congregated near the river in the summer. Betsie hummed a song as she jumped over a stone in the path, already planning the rides she would take, and estimating how much money she had and if Miriam would loan her some from her considerable savings.

The woods thinned, but Betsie heard the children before she saw them. Some were fishing a little up the river; a few adults in their *Rumspringa* were enjoying a picnic under a large tree. Betsie's friends were sitting by the edge of the river, their feet dangling in the water.

"You have feathers in your hair."

Betsie startled so badly she nearly lost her footing. Samuel King was sitting in the twisted roots of a nearby tree. He was fiddling with what looked like tiny rubber tires and strange metal wheels.

"What are you doing?" Betsie asked.

"I'm trying to make a toy car," Samuel said, his tongue sticking out as he concentrated. "You still have feathers in your hair."

"What?" Betsie brushed her hair absently. "I was in the chicken coop this morning."

Samuel said nothing. Betsie watched him fiddle for a while. Watching him work was fascinating. It was like solving a puzzle, his deft fingers twisting, bending, and detaching each piece as he felt for their right place in the toy's scheme.

"Betsie!" Susan called from near the water. "Betsie, come on!"

Betsie turned away reluctantly. Samuel glanced up at her. He shook his head.

"What?" Betsie asked, curious about what he was thinking.

Samuel got up and brushed the seat of his pants. He walked forward, and before Betsie knew what he was doing, he plucked a feather from Betsie's hair.

"You missed one," he said, placing the feather in her hand.

"Betsie!"

"I'm coming!" Betsie called. She turned around to thank Samuel, but he was jogging up the path into the woods. It was typical of Samuel to come where the rest of the village was gathered and keep his distance, like he wanted to be a part of them but lacked the courage to walk the three feet it would take to join them. A little annoyed by his hasty retreat, Betsie shrugged and joined her friends.

"Where have you been all day?" Susan asked.

"I was in town," Betsie said, taking off her shoes and socks, dipping her toes in the warm water. "I saw the circus," she smiled like the cat who ate the cream. "It's finally here."

"Too bad none of us will get to see it," little

Dolly Yoder said, chewing on a strand of her dark hair.

"Isn't your *Daed* taking you?" Betsie asked, feeling sympathy for the little girl.

"*Nee,*" Susan said, "you don't understand. None of our *Daeds* are taking us. The elders have forbidden it."

"What?" Betsie was shocked. The balloon of excitement that had been growing inside her popped, leaving a deflated husk in its place. "But why?"

"They said it was temptation," Dolly said.

Betsie looked around at the morose faces and a thought occurred to her. What if her friends were lying to her? Susan must have put them up to it to get back at Betsie for stealing her thunder the other day with the anaconda story.

"I'm going home," Betsie said, turning her nose up in the air. If this was how they were going to treat her, she would not play with them anymore. She ran all the way home till her lungs were on fire. She burst through the back door and bumped into Sarah.

"Where's the fire?" Sarah asked. Her eyes were puffy, and her face a little swollen. Betsie thought she might be ill.

"Did the elders forbid the circus?" Betsie

asked, gasping for breath as she clutched the stitch in her side. She searched for a smile, or a reassuring shake of the head, but Sarah's face was impassive.

"*Ja*, they did," Sarah said, folding a tea towel. "Miriam told me this morning."

"But why?" Betsie wailed. "Why would they do that?"

"They fear the circus will lead to temptation," Sarah said matter-of-factly, pulling out the risen dough from the cupboard nearest the oven.

"But that's ridiculous!"

"Not really," Sarah shrugged, stirring the contents of a saucepan on the stove. "We are forbidden to join in the town's Christmas celebrations. The principle is the same."

"That's different." Betsie stomped her foot.

"Is it really?" Sarah shouted, striking the spoon against the pan in anger. "Just because you want to go means we should change the rules?" Her eyes were blazing, her cheeks crimson. Betsie had never seen Sarah so angry. "Why does everything have to be about you, the way you want it? Life isn't fair, it's cruel and painful and the sooner you accept that the better for you."

Sarah burst into tears. She turned away so Betsie couldn't see her crying. Betsie rushed forward and hugged Sarah from behind. Her heart was hammering in her chest from the run and now from fright. Sarah, strong, wise Sarah, was crying like her heart was breaking and it was all Betsie's fault.

"I'm sorry, Sarah," Betsie sobbed. "I won't go to the circus. I won't even ask Ben to take us if he can't anymore."

Sarah cried harder at the mention of Ben. Footsteps came pattering into the kitchen from the living room. Miriam and Kathy separated the two sisters and set to drying tears.

"Sarah's just had a rough day," Kathy said, handing Betsie a glass of water. "Why don't you play outside with your friends for a few hours?"

Betsie didn't tell Kathy about leaving her friends, and she said nothing about the circus either, she was so guilt-ridden. But Betsie had seen how Sarah had reacted to Ben's name, and she had put two and two together. Something had gone wrong between Sarah and Ben. *Daed* must have found out because he had shouted at Sarah last night after dinner with George Lengacher.

Chewing her lip as she left the house to give Sarah the space she needed, Betsie formulated a plan. She was going to have to do it soon, and she would need help putting it into action. She thought of whom to confide in, running her hands through her hair. Something soft trailed her fingers. She stared at the small feather and Samuel King's pale face, screwed up in concentration over wheels, came to her mind.

It was time to pay Samuel King a visit.

DREAMS AND NIGHTMARES

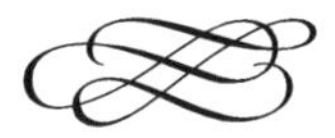

The cracks in the ceiling looked like claws. Samuel blinked. The house groaned and whined, settling for the night. Samuel whispered a prayer, and forced his mind to think of other things, pleasant things.

He thought of his latest project hidden under a loose floorboard near his dresser. There were still a few parts missing to get it to work. He would have to pay the junkyard a visit again. Old Rider Ness, the caretaker of the junkyard, let him sift through the old refrigerators and broken television sets for parts in exchange for cookies made by Samuel's mother, Selma King. She had made a fresh batch of rock cakes this morning, so Rider

Ness should be happy to let Samuel have his way for a few hours.

The floorboards creaked and Samuel glanced at his bedroom door. It was slightly ajar. He wasn't allowed a closed door after the hummingbird. Samuel had been eight then, and he had worked on a small toy bird he had found in the junkyard. Lifelike, with soft feathers that caught the light like rainbows, the bird had fascinated Samuel. He had replaced a few parts, wound the bird up, blew on it to make the tiny feathers ripple and let it go.

Selma had been delighted; Melvin had crushed the bird under his boot.

Samuel got up in bed and tiptoed over to the loose floorboard. He checked to make sure the warped wood wasn't visible. He couldn't risk Melvin finding out about the toy car he was working on, or the other mechanical toys he had fixed over the years.

He got back in bed, his thoughts heavy with his father's hatred of him. Samuel had tried to please him, he had tried to not think of the junkyard and the treasures it held, but he couldn't help it if he was good at fixing machines. It was a gift. He could look at gears and spokes and know how to fix it to make it work. It was like a puzzle he was very good at. But that wasn't the kind of son Melvin wanted.

He winced as he settled on his side. It got lonely in the house with only his mother's worry and his father's hatred. He was the only one who didn't have any siblings. He wondered if that was one of the reasons his father was so hard on him. Maybe if they had had another son, one more willing to work on the farm, and devoid of a passion for junkyard scraps, maybe things wouldn't be so bad.

Samuel's eyes grew heavy. He thought of the hummingbird and its rainbow feathers. His tired mind jumped from feathers to rich brown hair and Betsie Hershberger. A smile crossed his dozing face.

A sharp knock on his window made him jump out of bed, his bleary eyes trying to focus. His heart was galloping a mile a minute; his hackles were raised. He peered at the window. It was as if his dream had manifested into reality. Betsie Hershberger stood outside his window wearing the deepest frown he had ever seen on her face.

The house groaned as if it sensed her there. Samuel shot out of bed and opened the window as noiselessly as possible.

"What are you doing here?" he asked.

"I'm here to ask you to return a favor," Betsie said, a hint of superiority in her voice.

"What?"

"I've been standing up for you in school when I didn't have to," Betsie whispered harshly. "It's got me in a lot of trouble with Isaac Hilty. The way I see it, you owe me a favor."

Samuel thought of the lie he told to legitimize her story but thought it best not to mention it. She looked as if she was worried about something and wouldn't appreciate being reminded of that.

"What do you need?"

"I need to go into town tomorrow morning," Betsie said. "I need you to take me because I don't know where Ben works."

"Ben?" Samuel frowned. "Ben Lambright? He works at the McCarthy farm."

"Do you know where it is?"

"*Ja*." Samuel shrugged. "It's not too far from the junkyard. I'll take you."

"*Denke*," Betsie sighed, her frown disappearing and a smile lifting her lips. It was as if she had been relieved of a very heavy load. "I knew I could count on you." She punched his arm in comradeship.

Samuel winced and clutched his arm gingerly.

"Hah," Betsie laughed. "I guess I don't know my own strength."

He grinned, his face flushing. The floorboards creaked and Melvin's wracking cough disrupted the peace of night like a flock of pigeons fleeing from the cat in their midst. Betsie and Samuel stared at each other, their eyes wide. Samuel waved her away. She didn't need to be told twice. Samuel waited a moment to watch her sprinting away in the moonlit night before jumping into bed, his eyes shut tight.

For the hundredth time, Samuel wondered if his father could hear his heart beating inside his chest. He tried to keep his face serene when his bedroom door creaked open like a long drawn-out scream. He balled his trembling hands into fists and fought the urge to bite on his knuckles to stifle his whimpers. A shadow blocked out the moonlight.

Samuel pretended to be asleep, praying that his father would believe the deception.

TRIP TO TOWN

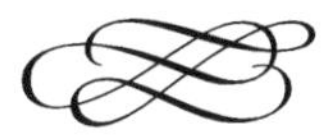

"Doesn't the junkyard smell?" Betsie asked.

"It does." Samuel nodded. "But I don't go there for fresh air."

Betsie laughed. She hadn't known Samuel King, the quiet, serious boy, would be so funny. It was the middle of the afternoon, a time when most children would be inside their homes and out of the sweltering sun, but Betsie had a mission and Samuel was going to help her with it.

She hadn't been sure Samuel would come. She had waited by the river for twenty minutes, convinced that she would have to trek to town alone and ask for directions to the McCarthy farm. She had just decided to leave when Samuel emerged from the trees.

It was surprisingly pleasant to talk to him. He wasn't boring or dumb. Samuel was smart and funny.

They came out on the town side of the woods. A house edged with pear trees was the marker that town had started. Samuel and Betsie were helping themselves to some pears when the screen door opened and two boys a few years older than them came out. They were dressed in *Englischer* clothes, denim jeans and sleeveless shirts, and their red hair was clipped close to their scalps.

"Hey," the older boy called. "You can't pick those. They're ours!"

"They're outside your fence," Betsie said, pocketing two pears in her apron pocket.

"But it's still our property," the boy spat.

"Come on, Ronan," the younger boy whined. "Let them have the stupid pears. We're late. They must have already washed the bear."

"Bear?" Betsie asked, intrigued. "What bear?"

"Dad was right. You plain people really know nothing, do you?" the boy named Ronan said. "The circus bear. They wash it and feed it every day before the performance in the big tent."

"There's an alley behind the library where you

can see it all," the younger boy said. His cheeks dimpled when he smiled.

"That's where the freaks pitched up their sleeping tents," Ronan said. "Come on, Jack. Let these two have the pears. We'll buy candy apples."

Betsie watched the brothers go with longing in her heart. If things had been different, she would have told that Ronan a thing or two about the circus and plain people's intelligence. But as things stood, she wasn't allowed to go. She felt bitterness flood her mouth, and she threw a pear over the fence and into the garden, where it bounced twice before coming to rest in the grass.

"This is so stupid." Betsie ground her teeth. "We should go to the circus too."

"No point in crying over spilled milk." Samuel shrugged. Betsie stared at him as if he had gone insane. "That's what my *Mamm* always says."

"I don't remember my mother," Betsie mumbled, and stomped off towards the road that led to the town center. She was angry at the unfairness of it all. She loved her village and wouldn't dream of any life other than within the community. Yet sometimes, when she heard Kathy talk about the movies, or how Miriam had taken so long to be baptized, she wondered if her sisters didn't feel it too, a twang of discord at the back of their minds.

Samuel finally caught up with her when they reached the town courthouse.

"I'm sorry about your *Mamm*," he said. There was a muted sincerity about Samuel. He didn't feel the need to resort to big gestures, or earnestly prove his loyalty. He had come when Betsie had called. That was all the action needed to prove he was a good friend.

"It was a long time ago." Betsie shook her head. "Plus, I have sisters to make up for it. They care for me just as well."

"I don't have siblings," Samuel said, polishing a pear with his handkerchief. "So I guess we're even."

Betsie smiled and felt her mood lifting.

"How far is the junkyard?"

"Not far." Samuel took a large bite out of his pear. "Twenty-minute walk from the hospital."

They crossed the main square through the throng of people going about their day. There were flyers for the circus everywhere they looked, and Betsie felt an anxious need to at least peek in at the circus. Surely, looking at it from afar wouldn't be breaking the rules.

They were passing the library when Betsie stopped.

"Can we go into the alley for a minute?" Betsie asked, chewing on her lip. "The bear might still be there."

Samuel stared at her. Betsie felt bad for suggesting it. This hadn't been the plan. She had asked him to take her to Ben, and now she was being greedy and selfish. She wouldn't be surprised if Samuel said no.

"Okay." Samuel shrugged. "If that's what you want."

Betsie nearly jumped for joy.

"I feel so bad." Betsie giggled.

"I know." Samuel grinned.

"What are you two doing?"

The bellow made them both jump. George Lengacher was striding towards them across the street. His thin beard quivered as he looked from one guilty face to the other and put two and two together.

"How dare you two? Going to the circus when it was expressly forbidden!"

"*Nee,* we weren't," Betsie said. "We were going to meet Ben Lambright on the Englischer farm."

"Do not make your situation worse by lying, young lady," George said, holding up a hand.

"Come with me now. I'm taking you both home." He took Betsie's hand and tugged her along behind him. Samuel fell in step.

Betsie glanced at Samuel. They were in big trouble now, and it was all her fault.

PUNISHMENT

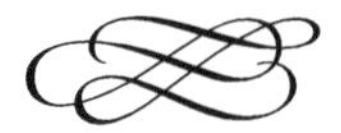

Gott was punishing her for being greedy. Betsie felt her insides burn with shame as she watched Samuel get out of the buggy behind George Lengacher. Melvin King was chopping wood across the yard, and Selma King was sitting in a chair on the porch with her mending basket. It was a large two-story house, and she wondered how three people lived in it without feeling dwarfed by its size. Melvin looked up from his stack of wood and wiped his forehead with a handkerchief. They were going to be very disappointed with Samuel, and Betsie was to blame.

Shame burned her throat, and hot tears threatened to fill her eyes. She had sinned, she had given into temptation, and *Gott* had struck her down before she could follow through with her wicked plan. She was willing to be punished for her sin, but she didn't want Samuel to suffer for her naughty behavior.

She hoped Melvin wasn't too hard on Samuel. He didn't have siblings like she did to protect her from their father's wrath, and so she hoped, him being an only child, he would have his parents' unconditional love. She wondered if Leroy would listen to the rest of his daughters this time or decide that this offence was too big to be swept under the rug without punishment.

Betsie absently watched Melvin come to meet George, as Selma got up from her chair. She was so lost in her own thoughts that when Melvin struck Samuel with his open hand, she thought she had imagined it. But then a second blow fell, and Samuel went down in the dirt.

"Stop!" Betsie screamed, scrambling out of the buggy. "Don't hurt him! It wasn't his fault."

George stopped Betsie mid-run. His skin was the color of whey and he was swallowing hard. Selma was holding back sobs on the porch. Melvin ran his hands through his disheveled hair, his face a forbidding mask of rage. Samuel got up and backed away a step, his head hanging low. Melvin took a threatening step forward.

"What were you thinking?" Melvin roared. "You've shamed me for the last time!"

Melvin raised his hand to strike.

"Melvin, wait," George bleated. "I, uh, I might have been mistaken."

"What?" Melvin asked, turning his sharp gaze on George, who trembled a little.

"I saw them near the library." George swallowed. "I, uh, I just assumed, I mean I thought they were going to the circus. But, er, the girl said they were going towards the McCarthy farm."

"Why were you going to the McCarthy farm?" Melvin jostled Samuel's shoulder. "Huh? Were you taking her to see that junkyard? Were you going to the junkyard, boy?"

"*Nee,* Melvin," George cried. "Let's hear the girl out."

"Please, Mr. King, sir," Betsie hiccoughed. "I wanted to see Ben Lambright because he made my sister cry. I didn't know the way, so I asked Samuel. We weren't going to see the circus, I promise!"

Melvin was breathing heavily, looking at Betsie with bulging, furious eyes. Betsie thought she would faint with fright if he didn't look away. Selma walked out into the yard and touched her husband's shoulder. He shrugged her off.

"Samuel is a good boy, Melvin," she whimpered. "He wouldn't go to the junkyard after you forbade it, would you, Samuel?"

"*Nee, Mamm,*" Samuel shook his head. His cheeks were red from where Melvin had struck him. "I'm sorry for the trouble, *Daed.*"

"There, see, the children are sorry." George tried to laugh it off, but it came across as a hoarse cough. "Let's forget this happened. It was a misunderstanding."

"Get out of my sight," Melvin snarled at Samuel, ignoring George. He picked up his axe and stalked to the back of the house. Samuel flinched but did as he was told. He walked towards his porch with Selma's arm around him. Melvin went back to chopping wood.

Betsie made to go to Samuel, but George pulled her back.

"I need to get you home," he said.

"But I have to apologize," Betsie said. "I have to tell Samuel I'm sorry."

"I'm sure he already knows," George said, dragging her to the buggy.

Betsie watched Selma wipe Samuel's face as the buggy pulled away. Samuel winced, but didn't cry. Betsie gasped, remembering punching him playfully on the arm the night before. She had thought she had hit him harder than she had intended, but what if he had a bruise on his arm? Looking at Melvin's forbidding figure at the chopping stump, and the blatant dislike he had for his son, she wouldn't be surprised if this wasn't the first time he had hit Samuel.

Betsie sobbed all the way home. She had never seen violence in her life. Leroy was often angry with her, but he had never lifted a finger to any of his daughters. But then again, none of his daughters had tried to go against the elders' express orders.

Would this be the straw that broke the camel's back? She knew Leroy thought her spoiled and coddled. He had been furious with her when she had agitated the bull. Would he consider this a mistake serious enough to be punished? Would he hit her like Samuel's father?

The thought made her blood run cold and her tears dried on her cheeks. She waited, in dread, till the buggy stopped in front of her home.

SHAME

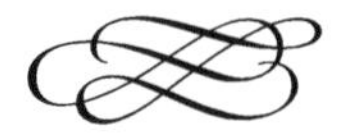

The clip-clop of the horses' hooves was perfectly synced with Betsie's heart. The house came into view and she looked at it as if she were seeing it for the first time. It was a single-story house, sprawled a little haphazardly with the air of being incomplete. The screen door in the back opened and Sarah emerged with a bucket of chicken feed. Betsie watched her sister stare at the sky and the knife of guilt twisted horribly.

Betsie had gone to town to talk to Ben, she had gone to help Sarah, but she had failed because of her own selfish greed.

"There you go," George said, parking the

buggy by the house. "If it's all right by you, I won't tell Leroy."

He wouldn't meet her eye. Melvin's behavior had affected him. The community didn't condone violence, and it went against the peaceful Amish nature. George was a frail old man, and he had always been kind. He respected Melvin's right to discipline his own son, but that did not mean he had to like it. By choosing not to tell Leroy of Betsie's attempts to see the circus, he was trying to do his part in preventing another harsh punishment.

But this didn't bring any peace to Betsie. She stepped off the buggy and stood in the yard for a while, watching George Lengacher's buggy disappear behind the bend in the path. She felt more guilt twist around her gut and squeeze it. Samuel's father slapped him twice just for accompanying her to town, yet she was being given the chance of no punishment at all. No, she would not let this injustice happen. After all, wasn't she always crying about how unfair things were? She was going to do the right thing.

Betsie went to the fields first but couldn't find Leroy. Then she went to the vegetable garden and then the apple orchard. She finally turned to the barn. It would fit to get her punishment in there if she found Leroy.

He was tending to the goats. The herd was riddled with worms and Leroy had spent the past two days deworming them. Betsie stood in the doorway for a few minutes watching her father work. He was so intent on the task at hand that he did not notice her.

Screwing up her courage, Betsie walked inside. The bull snorted and paw the ground, and Betsie flinched. Leroy looked up, his brown eyes finding Betsie in the gloom, and she felt her breath catch in her throat.

"Tell your sister I'll have lunch later," Leroy said dismissively.

"Sarah didn't send me," Betsie said in a small voice.

"What? Speak up," Leroy snapped.

"I said, Sarah didn't send me," Betsie said a bit more clearly.

"Then what do you want?" Leroy said, still not looking at her.

"I wanted to talk to you."

"Look, if this is about the bull, I forgive you."

"It's not about the bull." Betsie sucked on her lower lip and burst into tears.

Leroy stood up, taken aback by her reaction.

He quickly washed his hands, his eyes darting towards the barn door, his expression deeply uncomfortable as if he was hoping for one of his daughters to come and save him from the situation.

"Er, don't cry," he said. "What's wrong?"

"I did a horrible thing," Betsie wailed. "You're going to hate me."

"How can I hate you when I don't even know what you did?" Leroy raised his hands. Betsie cried louder. "Okay, I promise I won't hate you, okay? What did you do?"

"I went to town with Samuel King," Betsie hiccoughed.

"To see the circus?" Leroy asked sharply.

"*Nee… ja…* I mean not at first," Betsie said. "I wanted to talk to Ben, but…"

"Ben!" Leroy thundered. "Why did you want to meet him?"

Betsie's face grew hot. She wanted to kick herself for being so stupid. She had come to confess her sin of temptation and leading Samuel astray, but all she had done is make things worse for Sarah and Ben.

"I… I… *Daed,* I wanted to ask why he made Sarah cry," Betsie said, deciding to stick to her decision to tell the truth. No more telling lies for Betsie. They got her in more trouble than they were worth. "She's been miserable, and I know she loves him, and I hadn't expected this kind of behavior from him."

Leroy's eyes flickered and Betsie thought she saw a hint of shame in them.

"You've met him?" Leroy asked, his tone offhand.

"*Ja*. They walked me to school a few times."

"And you think he's worthy of Sarah?"

"*Ja*," Betsie nodded, shaking a teardrop off her chin and onto her apron. "Of course. Because he's just like you."

"What?" Leroy was shocked.

"He is," Betsie insisted. "He's proud and takes his responsibilities very seriously. Just like you."

"Is that why he works on an *Englischer* farm?" Leroy jeered.

"I asked him about that," Betsie said, "and he told me he doesn't want to be beholden to anyone in the community for his success. He wants to buy the lands next to his small inheritance so he can make a barn worthy of Sarah."

"Not beholden to the community?" Leroy sniffed. "The entire community is about supporting each other and helping in their time of need. If he isn't willing to accept support, he will not be willing to give it."

"But isn't that what you do, *Daed*?" Betsie asked in a small voice. "Every year we ask to help bring in the harvest but you refuse. You refuse the help of the community and run this entire farm by yourself, for us, your *dochders*. Ben is doing just the same."

Leroy looked at Betsie for a long time, as if he was finally seeing her as an individual person and not a blabbering baby.

"And what were you doing in town that made you come crying home?" he asked suddenly, taking Betsie by surprise.

"We were going to peek into the circus," Betsie said. "But George Lengacher caught us before we could. I still shouldn't have done it. Samuel's *Daed* hit him because I made him go, and I now understand what the elders meant by temptation being a sin. I'm sorry, *Daed*."

She had expected him to stomp around, kick a bucket, scream, and throw her in the bull's pen. She hadn't expected him to chuckle, then roar with laughter. The bull found this turn of events very disconcerting because it lowed in remorse at losing a chance to gore her.

"It's all right," Leroy said. "I'm not mad. It's the

circus, of course you'd be tempted, you who have always gotten what you wanted. As long as no one came to harm, there's nothing to worry about."

"But Samuel did come to harm," Betsie cried. "Mr. King slapped him twice and shook him!"

Leroy ran a hand through his beard. He looked like the news didn't come as a surprise to him.

"Melvin has always struggled with his anger," Leroy sighed. "He had a very strict father as well. But I had no idea he was hitting Samuel. No wonder that boy is so quiet and aloof."

Betsie felt blazing anger towards his parents, Melvin for treating Samuel this way, and Selma for allowing it.

Leroy read her face and gently touched her arm.

"Don't worry about Samuel or Sarah," he said. "I'll take care of it."

She smiled weakly. For the first time in her life, she felt pride in her father that she had only heard in the voices of her friends. Looking at Leroy's kind smile, she knew she could trust him to keep his promise. She turned to go back to the house. She suddenly felt drained of all energy and just wanted to curl up in bed and go to sleep.

AMENDS

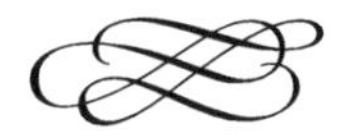

She didn't have a fever, nor was her throat sore. Sarah tucked Betsie in, collected the empty glass of milk, and left the room, wondering about Betsie's sudden lethargy and how puffy her eyes were. Had she been crying? But why?

"Sarah!" Kathy called from the front door. "I'm leaving. I won't be home till after dinner."

"Okay," Sarah called back.

She placed the dirty glass in the sink. Miriam was sitting at the kitchen table writing a letter.

Sarah loved all her sisters, especially Miriam. But there were times she felt she was being taken for granted. They had been too young when

Mamm died to really help her with any of the housework, then Miriam had developed an aversion to cooking, and Kathy had discovered the joys of *Rumspringa*. And Leroy let them all have their way. All except Sarah.

Sarah was expected to care for the house, no excuses. Even during her *Rumspringa* she was supposed to be at home during meal times to cook for the family. She hadn't had the luxury of a proper *Rumspringa* like her sisters. She had no time to spend on herself. The only thing she had found for herself, the one thing that gave her pleasure, was Ben, and even that had been snatched away from her.

Putting a few sandwiches on a plate, Sarah headed for the barn. If left to his own devices, Leroy would probably never eat lunch. It was her duty as a daughter to make sure he ate his meals. She found him sitting on a stool just inside the barn, a blade of grass in his mouth. He flashed her a big smile as she approached him.

"Lovely day," he said, but Sarah was in no mood to make conversation. She handed him his plate and turned to leave. "So when is his barn going to be ready?"

"Does it matter?" Sarah was sick and tired of

the baiting. Leroy had refused to have her married to Ben, so why drag this out?

"If you're going to marry this harvest season, it does," Leroy said matter-of-factly, biting into one of the sandwiches. "I won't have you sleeping under the stars."

"What?" Sarah was confused.

Leroy swallowed. He looked ashamed.

"I was wrong," he mumbled. "About Ben. I was looking at him from the aspect of a man who owns his own barn, his own fields. I didn't even try to understand the motive behind his actions. I judged him quickly and harshly, and I judged you for choosing him. I'm sorry."

Sarah stared, her mouth wide open. What miracle had taken place for her father to change his staunch beliefs in the space of thirty-six hours?

"Do you mean it?" Sarah asked. "You're okay with Ben and me getting married?"

"*Ja, dochder,*" Leroy said. "It's the least I can do after you helped me keep this family functioning after your *Mamm* passed away. I couldn't have done any of this without you."

Sarah burst into tears. She was so happy words failed her.

"Oh, *nee*," Leroy moaned. "Not another one. What is it with my *dochders* and crying? I just gave you joyful news."

"*Denke, Daed*," Sarah said, throwing herself in her father's arms and holding him tightly.

THE HEART OF INNOCENCE

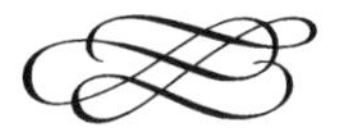

Betsie was all alone. Kathy and Miriam had camped on her bed and told her a few stories before retiring to bed themselves. Betsie was finally alone with her thoughts, thoughts that twisted and turned over how her thoughtless actions had gotten Samuel in trouble.

A sudden knock on her window made her sit upright, holding her covers to her face. Had Melvin found out about Leroy's leniency and come to punish her instead?

It was Samuel, waving at her to open the sash. Betsie rushed over and lifted the window sash. The night air was fragrant and pleasant compared to the heat of the day.

"I'm sorry, Samuel."

"You don't have to be." He shrugged.

"You got hit because of me," she insisted.

"*Nee.*" He shook his head. "He would have done it anyway. He only needs a paltry excuse to get angry."

"Why does he do it? Doesn't he know it's wrong?"

"I'm not the son he wanted." Samuel shrugged. "I'm not athletic. I don't have any interest in farming or animal husbandry. I wish to learn about mechanics and build machines. I'm strange and nothing like he wanted." The notes of bitterness were distinct in his tone. "That's why he hates me." Fat tears pooled in Samuel's eyes. He brushed them away with fisted fingers.

"No one deserves this." Betsie held his hand. "And you're not strange. You're special. You have a gift from *Gott*. You just need to find a way to make it work in our Old Order community. You're kind and generous, you're loyal and a good friend. And if your father can't see that, then... you don't need him. You have me. I'll be your friend."

Samuel's smile turned into a wince. He chuckled, holding the side of his face that must still hurt from the slap he had gotten earlier.

"Then this was worth it," Samuel said, punching Betsie lightly on the arm.

She grinned like a fool.

"BETSIE! BREAKFAST!" Kathy called down the hall.

Betsie rubbed her tired eyes. She had spent half the night talking to Samuel. He had finally left a few hours before dawn, but Betsie had been too excited to go to sleep immediately. She had read a book till dawn and had only gotten two hours of sleep.

She sat at the table, her eyelids heavy with sleep. Sarah placed a large stack of pancakes smothered in butter and honey in front of her, then kissed her forehead. Betsie stared.

"What was that for?" she asked.

Leroy laughed from across the table.

"I told you I'd fix it," he said.

Sarah hummed as she went about the kitchen. It was a sight for sore eyes. Betsie bit into her pancakes, the sweet honey coating the roof of her mouth. Things were finally falling back into place, and she vowed never to disrupt them again with her selfishness.

"More pancakes?" Sarah asked.

"Yes, please," Betsie cried.
Life was good again.

EPILOGUE

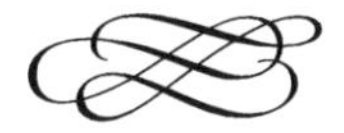

The barn was too small to accommodate everyone, so half the tables had to be set outside. Betsie didn't mind. She served casseroles and bread with Miriam, Kathy, and half the community that had come to help.

The Lambright family was large and very close. They had prepared all the food to help out. Betsie thought they were very tactful to take up the job without making Miriam feel like a horrible sister for not being able to cook for her sister's wedding feast.

"She looks lovely," Kathy sniffed.

"And happy," Miriam agreed.

Sarah, dressed in her wedding gown of deep purple, looked radiant. Ben looked very handsome. He couldn't take his eyes off his bride. Betsie watched with the rest as the food was cleared and the dancing began. They glided gracefully across the floor, the picture of the fairytales Miriam used to read to her when she was younger.

"Beautiful Betsie," Ben approached her after a while. "Care to dance?"

"My feet are killing me," Sarah complained, taking a seat at one of the tables.

Betsie danced with Ben, then laughed when Leroy cut in.

"You've already taken Sarah," he joked. "You're not taking Betsie."

"Somebody will," Ben laughed.

"Not anytime soon," Betsie cried and ran to meet her friends.

Samuel was keeping his distance from the rest of the children, as usual. Betsie made a beeline for him with a large plate of cookies.

"Meet me in the green room!" she whispered, "And bring milk!"

She ran off without waiting for him, her high spirits thrilling at the joy of the day. Her eldest sister was marrying the man she loved, Miriam was being courted by Nathan Zook, and Kathy was being courted by no less than three young men, so popular was she in the village. Leroy had gone back to being the absent father, but now his daughters knew they could rely on him when they needed him.

Betsie ran into the edge of the woods where a patch of ivy had gone wild. Left unattended in the woods, it had covered an entire tree. The children of the village liked to call it the green room and often went there to play hide and seek.

Betsie sat down and waited patiently for Samuel to show up. He arrived five minutes later with two tall glasses of milk in his hands. He walked carefully so he wouldn't drop any. They settled on the dry leaves and tucked into the cookies and milk.

"I can't wait to be married," Betsie said. "I'll have many children, and they will get cookies and milk every day!"

"I will have my own room for my toys and machines." Samuel looked wistfully up in the canopy of drying leaves.

"And pancakes for breakfast."

"And books, lots of books."

"And roast chicken, and cheese toast!"

"Your children will have horrible tummy aches." Samuel laughed.

"And your children will have headaches!" Betsie giggled.

They broke the last cookie in half and shared it. When the crumbs had been swept away and the last of the milk drained, they settled against the trunk of the tree, their hands resting on their stomachs, content.

"Betsie."

"Hmm?"

"I wanted to thank you."

"I'll get you more cookies from the pantry."

"*Nee,* it wasn't for the cookies. One of the elders came to our house a few weeks ago. Saul Yoder. He talked to my *Daed* about the hitting. He told him it was against the community. My *Daed* was angry. He told Mr. Yoder that what he did with his family was none of the elders' business, but Mr. Yoder insisted that if *Daed* didn't stop, they'd have to consider taking action. Someone comes and checks on me twice a month now. *Daed* doesn't like it, but there isn't anything he can do about it."

Betsie hadn't known that the day would have gotten better somehow, but it had. Everything had fallen in place, and the niggling worry that she had had about Samuel's well-being was also satisfied.

"But why are you thanking me?" Betsie asked. "I did nothing."

"*Daed* is convinced that it was George Lengacher who told the elders." Samuel grinned. "But I didn't think Mr. Lengacher had it in him. So I asked Mr. Yoder how he found out, and he told me it was your *Daed.* He had talked to them about it after you told him. So thank you."

"You're my friend." Betsie punched Samuel in the arm, delighted when he didn't wince. "That's what friends do."

"I'm still new to the friendship thing." Samuel chuckled.

"You won't be for long," Betsie said. "Tag!" She punched him again and ran.

Samuel sat bewildered for a moment till he caught on to what was happening. Betsie shrieked with delight as she ran back to the party, her friend racing after her. The sun sank below the horizon, but the wedding party went on late into the night.

Click here to get notification when the next book is available, and to hear about other good things I give my readers (or copy and paste this link into your browser: *bit.ly/Grace-FreeBook*). **You will also receive a free copy of *Secret Love* and *River Blessings*, exclusive spinoffs from the *Amish Hearts* and the *Amish Sisters series*** for members of my Readers' Group. These stories are NOT available anywhere else.

FREE DOWNLOAD

EXCLUSIVE and FREE for subscribers of my Readers' Group

CLICK HERE!

amazonkindle

NOTE FROM THE AUTHOR

Thank you for taking a chance on *The Heart of Innocence,* Book 1 of the *Amish Hearts* series.

Did you enjoy the book? I hope so, and I would really appreciate it if you would help others enjoy this book, and help spread the word.

Please consider leaving a review today telling other readers why you liked this book, wherever you purchased this book, or on Goodreads. **It doesn't need to be long**, just a few sentences can make a huge difference. **Your reviews go a long way in helping others discover what I am writing**, and decide if a book is for them.

I appreciate anything you can do to help, and if you do write a review, wherever it is, please send an email at grace@gracelewisauthor.com, so I could thank you personally.

Here are some places where you can leave a review:

- Amazon.com;
- Goodreads.

Thank you for reading, and have a lovely day,

Grace Lewis

PS: I love hearing from my readers. Feel free to email me directly at grace@gracelewisauthor.com (or to connect with me on Facebook here https://www.facebook.com/GraceLewisAuthor). I read and respond to every message.

THE HEART OF LONGING – AMISH HEARTS SERIES, BOOK 2 (EXCERPT)

SUMMARY

Torn between the choice of stepping out with her best friend or the handsome new man in the village, Betsie Hershberger must come to terms with her desires, and the nature of her own wild heart.

Betsie Hershberger's Rumspringa is full of surprises. Kathy is getting married, Sarah is having her third child, and Miriam is thinking of leaving the nest but not in the conventional way. And no sooner does Betsie start her *Rumspringa* than Samuel King, her childhood friend, asks her to walk out with him. But a new man in the village has caught her eye, and she is sure she has caught his.

Must she sacrifice her heart's desire to keep her childhood friendship, or will she follow her heart and find happiness?

>> Copy and paste this link: *bit.ly/GL-Longing* into your browser to read it now.

CHAPTER ONE

It was the last warm day of the year before fall took hold. The rust-colored leaves were still clinging to their branches, loath to let go. Under the canopy of dying leaves, a new life was being celebrated.

The freshly painted barn still smelled of varnish mingled with the scent of sweet hay. Mouth-watering food made the trestle tables groan, while the air was thick with music and the laughter of children.

"Careful!" Betsie Hershberger dodged in time. Eli, her four-year-old nephew, went whizzing past her skirts, closely followed by Amos, his younger brother. Betsie watched their flaxen heads weave through legs and disappear behind one of the tables. She adjusted the tray of hot *kaffe* mugs in her hands and continued to serve.

"Kathy looks so happy," Anna Lambright cooed. "I don't think I've ever seen such a beautiful bride."

Betsie glanced at the table across the yard. Kathy Fisher née Hershberger was dressed in a simple dress of inky blue that brought out the color of her eyes. Betsie recalled the long nights spent gossiping and teasing Kathy as she lovingly stitched her wedding dress. Kathy was the undisputed beauty of the Hershberger girls. Her natural good looks were reminiscent of Audrey Hepburn. Sitting next to her husband, Ivan Fisher, she looked fairly radiant.

"None for you." Betsie pulled the tray back when Sarah Lambright, the eldest Hershberger girl, tried to take a mug.

"Oh, I can't wait to have this baby," Sarah grumbled, folding her arms on top of her burgeoning belly.

"May *Gott* grant you a girl this time." Anna, her sister-in-law, giggled. "My brothers are just as much fools for sons as our father was. Granted, Ben has done better than the rest."

Sarah blushed with pleasure. The Lambright men were notorious for having sons and lacking the fortitude needed to leave their lands to only one. The generosity of spirit and abundance of sons had dwindled the vast Lambright holdings into small Lambright pockets across the village, forcing many Lambright men to sell and seek their fortune in other Amish villages. Ben Lambright, Sarah's husband, had been left a plot no bigger than a vegetable garden. He had worked with *Englischer* farmers till he could buy the adjoining fields and land for a barn, effectively making his the largest Lambright farm in the village. Sarah was very proud of her Ben.

"I wouldn't mind a little girl." Sarah patted her belly. "Eli and Amos are a handful. *Gott* have mercy on me if it's another boy."

The women laughed. The mugs all gone, Betsie headed back to the kitchens to fetch more *kaffe*.

"It's going well?" Eva Fisher, mother of the groom, asked, taking out another leek casserole from the oven. A tiny woman, she had grown wider instead of inching taller. Wide-lined face, with a wide-lined nose, she reminded Betsie of rocks piled on top of each other: harsh, jagged, sloping. There was nothing soft about her body. Yet, when Eva took you in her arms, her flesh radiated warmth, like stones left out in the sun, because the softness lived inside her: in her eyes, her smiles, and her loving heart.

"*Ja,* Mrs. Fisher." Betsie wiped the sweat off her brow. "We need more *kaffe.*"

"*Kaffe,*" Eva sighed. "The Amish and their *kaffe*. If you don't put a stop to it, that's all they'll be drinking."

"You love it too." Betsie giggled.

"*Ja,* I do." Eva laughed. "Go on then."

Betsie filled a pan with water and placed it on the stove. Fisher women and Lambright girls kept going in and out of the kitchen, lending a hand, tossing salads, and mixing sauces. Eva supervised it all like a mother hen. Not having known her mother, Betsie found Eva's nurturing nature endearing, and again thought how lucky Kathy was to be her daughter-in-law.

She was pouring the *kaffe* in mugs when Nancy Schwartz sidled up beside her.

"So." Nancy wiggled her eyebrows. "I hear you're walking out with Samuel King."

Betsie swallowed the tirade of explanations that always threatened to burst out of her mouth whenever anyone asked her about Samuel. She didn't understand why she felt the need to provide explanations for her choice to say yes to him. He was kind, sweet and had been her friend for five years. Of course, she had said yes when he had asked her to go for a buggy ride. Why would she say no?

She immediately silenced the voices in her head, giving the answers to that question.

"*Ja,*" she said shortly, busying herself with her task.

"I must admit, I never pictured you with someone like him." Nancy swiped an apple off a fruit bowl and bit into it. The ripping of the fruit's flesh grated on Betsie's nerves. "He's just so..." Nancy waved her apple around, searching for a word. "It's like his head is in another place, do you know what I mean?"

"Probably meditating on the glory of *Gott.*" Betsie shrugged, trying to hide her annoyance.

Nancy snorted.

"Thinking of another crazy invention, more like." Nancy laughed. "Are you really walking out with him?"

Betsie nodded tightly. She picked up the tray, signaling that the conversation was over.

"Well, at least you are walking out, and only a month into your *Rumspringa.*" Nancy sighed, her florid cheeks deflating a little. "It's been a whole year of *Rumspringa* and I haven't walked out with anyone."

If Nancy had been a little kinder, Betsie might

have felt sorry for her. As things were, she felt a mean satisfaction, but shame was fast on its heels. Betsie put the tray down and placed a comforting hand on Nancy's shoulder.

"You're only seventeen," she said. "Things will get better."

"You think so?" Nancy tilted her head; the desire to believe Betsie was bright in her mud-colored eyes. "Or will I turn out to be like Miriam, teaching other people's children and running after my nephews at my sister's wedding? Is it true she can't cook to save her life?"

By sheer force of will, Betsie stopped herself from digging her fingernails into Nancy's fleshy shoulder. Fuming, she picked up the tray and marched out before the urge to throw boiling *kaffe* in Nancy's bloated face won out over her restraint.

Making fun of Samuel was one thing, but Nancy had crossed a line talking about her sister Miriam that way. People in the village didn't understand things that were different from them. And Miriam and Samuel were different.

Miriam refused to cook, not because she couldn't but because she didn't want to. Approached to walk out a few times, Miriam had refused each suitor, not having any desire to marry. She loved to teach, and could have spent all day at the school if the pupils didn't have to go home.

Samuel loved machinery, an unheard-of thing in an Old Order community. He could fix the rudimentary pulley systems across the village in seconds and had a collection of gadgets he had made from scraps from the junkyard under his bedroom floorboards.

They were both considered odd, and Betsie guessed it was this oddity in Samuel that she liked best because it reminded her of Miriam.

Yet…

Betsie weaved through the crowd, offering *kaffe* to everyone, her mind deep in thoughts of Samuel and why she had agreed to walk out with him when she hadn't really wanted to. She hadn't ever thought of Samuel romantically, so when he had asked her to go for a buggy ride she had thought nothing of it, thinking it would be a platonic ride to town. When Samuel had shown up with a bunch of freshly picked flowers, her mistake in understanding him finally hit her. But by then it was too late.

"Would you like to dance?" Ben Lambright asked as she passed by the barn floor. "You have had no opportunity for fun all day."

"Just have to serve this last batch of *kaffe*." Betsie grinned. She turned to walk to the men seated at the far side of the barn but stopped. "Ben. Why don't you ask Nancy to dance?"

"Nancy Schwartz?"

"*Ja*. She looks like she'd like to dance if someone were to ask her. Go on," she urged. "It will make her day. And I want everyone to be happy on Kathy's big day."

Ben scouted for Nancy and found her on the far side, leaning against the wall, watching the dancing couples. He nodded to Betsie and maneuvered his way towards Nancy. Betsie served *kaffe* but her attention was on Nancy and Ben dancing, so she didn't hear the pattering feet or the tiny running figures coming in her path.

"Coming through!"

Eli ran past Betsie again, his giggles high-pitched. Betsie managed to steady herself.

"Coma thoo!"

Amos, always one step behind Eli, charged for her legs.

"Amos, *nee*!" Betsie cried.

"Careful!" someone else said.

Betsie braced herself for impact, her eyes shut tight in anticipation of the crash and tinkle of mugs. But there was no collision. The tray was firmly in her hands. Betsie opened her eyes to find Amos lifted up in the air, his shrieks of delight bringing a smile on every face. The man holding him up had his back to Betsie, but she could see his powerful arms and broad shoulders.

"You nearly did the pretty miss an injury," the man said. He had a pleasant voice, laced with warmth.

"I sorry, *Ant* Besthie," Amos lisped.

"It's okay," Betsie said, distracted by the man who had turned around. She had never seen him before in the village. He was remarkably handsome. His smile was striking, showing even white teeth. "*Denke.*"

"It was my pleasure," the man said. He looked to be in his mid-twenties, his strawberry blond hair just reaching the nape of his neck. He had a frank gaze that made Betsie's cheeks blaze involuntarily. "I'm Caleb; Caleb Nolt. I'm new around here. Ivan was kind enough to invite me to his wedding."

"Are you a friend of Ivan's?" Betsie asked, casually.

"Neighbor," Caleb said. "But I hope to be a friend soon. I might be wrong, but you look remarkably like Ivan's bride, Kathy."

"She's my sister. I'm Betsie. Betsie Hershberger."

"Pleased to make your acquaintance, Betsie."

She had the strangest tingling sensation in her belly hearing her name on his lips.

"Are you staying in Jamesport long?"

"I was hoping to make a home here." His smile was infectious. Betsie's stomach was full of butterflies. "My village in Indiana was moving away from the Old Order, and since I wasn't ready to move with them, I moved away."

"That must have been hard for you."

"*Ja*." Caleb nodded. "But I have found this village, and I hope I can serve it well."

"Welcome to our village," Betsie said. "I hope you find the peace you are looking for."

"I'm confident that I will," he said with a meaningful nod, and Betsie's heart began to beat a step faster.

She made to turn, but Caleb shot his hand out. Betsie gasped, thinking he was trying to grab her arm to make her stop. When he picked up a mug of *kaffe* instead, chuckling knowingly, her entire face flushed crimson, and she felt waves of embarrassment radiate off of her like heat.

Flustered, Betsie made it back to the kitchen, half the *kaffe* cups still on her tray.

"They've had enough of *kaffe* then?" Eva asked.

"Huh? Oh, *ja*."

"Are you all right?" Eva asked, placing a cool hand on Betsie's forehead. "You look feverish."

"I'm fine." Betsie shook her head and tried to smile reassuringly. "Just feeling a little lightheaded."

"You haven't had a bite since dawn." Eva tut-tutted. "Here, eat this."

She thrust a plate of roasted chicken and mashed potatoes in Betsie's hands. But Betsie had no appetite. She kept picturing that knowing smile, and her own mouth responded. She realized she must look foolish, food in her hands, smiling at nothing, her eyes glazed, her cheeks pink. She shook her head and forced herself to eat a little while her mind whirled about with possibilities.

Had she read that smile right? Caleb had shown clearly that he found her charming, worthy of his interest. And she had to admit she felt the same way. She didn't know him like Samuel, but she felt a keen desire to find out everything about him. He was Ivan's neighbor, that much she knew; he had moved to Jamesport because it was conservative like he wanted it. But this wasn't enough information.

She wanted to know where he had come from, what family he came from, his favorite food, his favorite color, the hymn he liked to sing while working in the field, and the passage of the Bible he related to most. She wanted to know all this and more.

Chewing on her chicken, the thought struck her that she knew none of these things about Samuel, and worse still, that she didn't care to know.

Betsie swallowed with difficulty, her throat suddenly parched.

OTHER BOOKS BY GRACE LEWIS

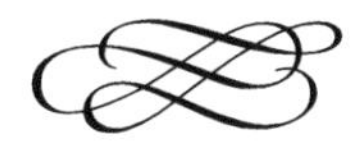

Click here to browse all Grace Lewis's Books (or copy and paste this link into your browser: *bit.ly/gracelewisauthor*).

THE AMISH HEARTS SERIES (PREQUEL TO THE AMISH SISTERS SERIES)

The Heart of Innocence, Book 1

Jamesport, Missouri, early 1980s.

Betsie Hershberger's whole world is her little Amish village and her small family. The youngest of four sisters, she is the apple of their eye, and privy to all their secrets. When the circus comes to town, Betsie's overactive imagination risks getting her eldest sister in trouble, and harming an innocent friend.

Sarah Hershberger is responsible for her sisters since their mother's death. Her father, Leroy, relies on her to keep track of the house and his willful daughters while he works on the farm, but Sarah fears this dependence will leave no room for her to make a family of her own. Proving this fear well founded, Leroy detests the only man Sarah loves and forbids marriage.

Will Betsie save the day? Will Sarah convince her father to grant her the love she seeks? Or will the sisters end up in more trouble than they bargained for?

>> Copy and paste this link: *bit.ly/GL-Innocence* into your browser to read it now.

The Heart of Longing, Book 2

Torn between the choice of stepping out with her best friend or the handsome new man in the village, Betsie Hershberger must come to terms with her desires, and the nature of her own wild heart.

Betsie Hershberger's Rumspringa is full of surprises. Kathy is getting married, Sarah is having her third child, and Miriam is thinking of leaving the nest but not in the conventional way. And no sooner does Betsie start her *Rumspringa* than Samuel King, her childhood friend, asks her to walk out with him. But a new man in the village has caught her eye, and she is sure she has caught his.

Must she sacrifice her heart's desire to keep

her childhood friendship, or will she follow her heart and find happiness?

>> **Copy and paste this link:** ***bit.ly/GL-Longing*** **into your browser to read it now.**

The Heart of Perseverance, Book 3

After three years of courtship, Betsie Hershberger wants to get married, but it doesn't look like Samuel King is going to propose anytime soon. Frustrated with his lack of commitment, Betsie is thinking of finding someone else. But when her father expresses the same wish and presents her with two suitors, Betsie is conflicted about what to do.

Samuel wants to marry Betsie, but he has problems at home that need his attention. His mother is very ill and needs treatment that his father refuses to let her get. His earnings in the village aren't enough, and the job in town goes against the Amish way.

With one thing going wrong after another, will Samuel and Betsie ever be able to reconcile their love and get married?

>> **Copy and paste this link:** ***bit.ly/GL-Perseverance*** **into your browser to read it now.**

Secret Love, exclusive book for members of my readers' list

Things come easy to Kathy, except love. The man she loves seems devoted to someone else. Will she have the courage to express her feelings, or is she destined to watch him marry someone else?

Ivan Fisher is twenty-two. He is the youngest son and the shortest, and he is conscious of his height. He is in love with Kathy Hershberger, but so is everyone else. He believes she is too good for him, so he picks Bertha Lapp to walk out with.

Kathy Hershberger doesn't mind the attention, but she feels despondent because the only man she likes has eyes for another. She is devastated when Ivan walks out with Bertha.

Will the two ever confess their love for each other, or are they destined to hold their love as a secret?

>> Copy and paste this link into your browser: *bit.ly/Grace-FreeBook* to read it now.

Complete Series Boxset

The whole *Amish Sisters* series is now available in a boxset: **Copy and paste this link: *bit.ly/ AmishSisters* into your browser to read it now.**

You can also read each book separately:

The Choice, Book 1 (excerpt)

Baptized into the Amish faith, Emma finds her heart divided between family, community and forbidden love for an *Englischer* man.

Emma King is a respectful and hard-working Amish girl. It is no wonder that she has caught the eye of Luke Yoder, one of the most upstanding men in the Amish community. Her sister Rachel, by comparison, is reckless and foolish; she risks bringing the family shame. Yet all of this is nothing compared to the Amish community's censure of her father, Samuel King, a man with an obsession. But Emma has secrets of her own: mistrust of Luke Yoder, and a growing attraction to a stranger… an *Englischer* man.

Facing the accusations of her community, and the disquiet of her own heart, Emma King must make a choice that might devastate her happy Amish life. Will she follow her heart, or surrender herself to the will of *Gott*?

>> Copy and paste this link: *bit.ly/GL-AmishChoice* into your browser to read *The Choice* now.

Faith, Book 2

Three Amish women, three tests of faith. Will they persevere in their love for *Gott* or will their hardships harden them to *Gott*'s benevolence?

Nestled in an Amish village, surrounded by friends, the King family is living the ideal life. Then sorrow comes to roost as one by one the pillars of the household are devastated.

Betsie King, severely ill, must rely on the help of her daughters and decide between her own mortality and the welfare of her family. Rachel must face her own sins and find redemption in the face of rejection. Emma has to deal with the dark secret of the man she is walking out with.

Will Betsie choose family over faith? Will Rachel redeem herself in the eyes of *Gott*? Will Emma be able to forgive Luke his human failings? Or will these trial tear the King family apart?

>> Copy and paste this link: *bit.ly/GL-AmishFaith* into your browser to read *Faith* now.

Heartache, Book 3

The King sisters' have come a long way, but life isn't done throwing them obstacles in their path. While Rachel must find the man who will make her happy, Emma must overcome the daunting risks to her unborn child.

When Emma Yoder discovers she is pregnant with her first child, she feels like *Gott* has granted her every blessing she has ever wished for. Safe in the cocoon of her husband's adoration and her family's love, Emma is looking forward to motherhood. But a friend's miscarriage and her own checkup at the *Englischer* hospital turn her dreams into a nightmare.

A temporary teaching position at the local Amish school has become a boon for Rachel King. She enjoys teaching and loves the children, especially Elijah Lapp, a motherless child whose neglectful Aunt can't seem to fill the void. Walking out with a man she finds annoying, Rachel finds herself hoping for the attentions of Elijah's father, but her past has a nasty way of catching up with her.

Will the two sisters overcome their hardships with the support of their families and the grace of *Gott,* or will their heartache engulf their peace of mind and happiness?

>> Copy and paste this link: *bit.ly/AmishHeartache* into your browser to read *Heartache* now.

Torment, book 4

Emma Yoder's life is perfect. She has two children and another one on the way. She is married to the man of her dreams, and she is the darling of the village. But a tragic accident threatens to tear this blissful life asunder. Losing all hope and support from the community, Emma faces the toughest decision of her life.

Will Emma be able to pull her happiness out of the maws of death?

Rachel Lapp is worried for her sister Emma, but her own personal loss is too great to bear. Married for four years without a child, Rachel craves a *boppli* above all else. Her obsession has driven her to consider *Englischer* methods that might estrange her from the community but it is a risk Rachel is willing to take.

Is Rachel willing to lose everything, the love and support of family, husband and community for a chance at motherhood?

A drought threatens the village and Samuel King's pushes his solar panel powered machines as the only solution to the Old Order community. Though the community is against these advancements Samuel believes they are the only way forward.

Will Samuel's obsession with technology spell doom and shunning for the entire family?

>> Copy and paste this link: *bit.ly/GL-AmishTorment* into your browser to read *Torment* now.

River Blessings, exclusive book for members of my readers' list

When the river blesses the King twins with its bounty the twins must go on a journey to find those *Gott* has deemed deserving of them.

When the King twins find a sack full of stray puppies in the river, they know it to be a sign from *Gott*. Thus begins a quest to find homes for the dogs, but there are obstacles along the way: angry adults, haunted houses and bitter hearts. Will the twins find their furry friends new homes, or will they have to give them up to the *Englischer* dog shelter?

>> **Copy and paste this link into your browser: *bit.ly/Grace-FreeBook* to read it now.**

This book is a work of fiction. Names, characters and places are either products of the author's imagination or used fictitiously. Any resemblance to actual persons, living or dead, events, locales or Amish communities is entirely coincidental. The author has taken liberties with locales, including the creation of fictional towns and places, as a mean of creating the necessary circumstances for the story. This books is intended for fictional purposes only, it is not a handbook on the Amish.

Manufactured by Amazon.ca
Bolton, ON